D0604037

Published by The Child's World®
1980 Lookout Drive • Mankato, MN 56003-1705
800-599-READ • www.childsworld.com

ACKNOWLEDGMENTS
The Child's World®: Mary Berendes, Publishing Director
The Design Lab: Kathleen Petelinsek, Design and Page Production
Literacy Consultants: Cecilia Minden, PhD, and Joanne Meier, PhD

LIBRARY OF CONGRESS
CATALOGING-IN-PUBLICATION DATA
Moncure, Jane Belk.
  My "g" sound box / by Jane Belk Moncure ;
illustrated by Rebecca Thornburgh.
    p. cm. — (Sound box books)
  Summary: "Little g has an adventure with items beginning with
her letter's sound, such as grapes, grass, goats, a goose, and a
gorilla in goggles."—Provided by publisher.
  ISBN 978-1-60253-147-5 (library bound : alk. paper)
  [1. Alphabet.] I. Thornburgh, Rebecca McKillip, ill. II. Title.
  PZ7.M739Myg 2009
  411—dc22   2008033163

Copyright ©2009 by The Child's World®
All rights reserved. No part of the book may be reproduced or
utilized in any form or by any means without written permission
from the publisher.

Printed in the United States of America • Mankato, MN
May, 2013 • PA02185

A NOTE TO PARENTS AND EDUCATORS:

Magic moon machines and five fat frogs are just a few of the fun things you can share with children by reading books with them. Reading aloud helps children in so many ways! It introduces them to new words, motivates them to develop their own reading skills, and expands their attention span and listening abilities. So it's important to find time each day to share a book or two . . . or three!

As you read with young children, you can help develop their understanding of how print works by talking about the parts of the book—the cover, the title, the illustrations, and the words that tell the story. As you read, use your finger to point to each word, modeling a gentle sweep from left to right.

Simple word games help develop important prereading skills, including an understanding of rhyme and alliteration (when words share the same beginning sound, such as "six" and "sand"). Try playing with words from a book you've just shared: "What other words start with the same sound as moon?" "Cat and hat, do those words rhyme?" The possibilities are endless—and so are the rewards!

Moncure, Jane Belk.
My "g" sound box /

c2009.
33305230490199
ca   03/24/14

My "g" Sound Box®

(This book uses only the hard "g" sound in the story line. Blends are included.
Words beginning with the soft "g" sound are included at the end of the book.)

WRITTEN BY JANE BELK MONCURE

ILLUSTRATED BY REBECCA THORNBURGH

Little  had a box. "I will find things that begin with my **g** sound," she said. "I will put them into my sound box."

Little  opened the gate and

went into the garden.

Little 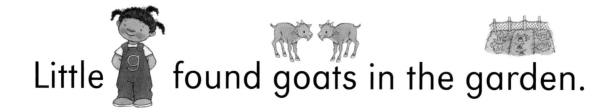 found goats in the garden.

Did she put the goats into her 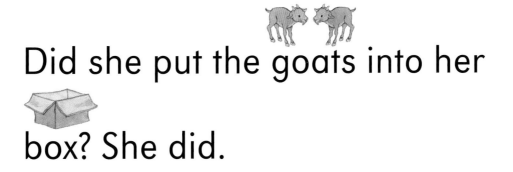 box? She did.

Then Little  found grass, lots

and lots of green grass.

She put some green grass into the box with the goats. But the goats ate it all up!

Little  found grapes, lots

and lots of grapes.

She put the grapes into the box.

But the goats ate up all the

grapes, too!

What could Little  do? She
found a gorilla.

She put the gorilla into the box
with the goats. Did the goats
eat the gorilla? No.

The goats grinned. The gorilla

grinned, too.

Little  found a guitar. She played the guitar. The gorilla danced.

Then the goats danced with
the gorilla.

Everyone giggled!

Little 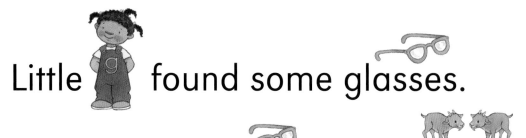 found some glasses.

She put the glasses on the goats.

Then she found goggles. She  put the goggles on the gorilla.

Just then, a goose and a gander

walked by.

"What funny goats! What a funny gorilla!" said the goose and gander.

Little  caught the goose

and gander.

"You belong in my sound box,"

she said.

The goose got into the box all by herself. "I will give you a gift," she said.

Then the goose laid an egg made of gold. All of it was gold!

Little  looked around her garden.

Little g's Word List

gander

garden

gate

gift

glasses

goat

goggles

gold

goose

gorilla

grapes

grass

guitar

Other Words with the Hard "g" Sound

ghost

glass

glove

glue

goldfish

gopher

grapefruit

gravy

grill

gum

gumdrop

Words with the Soft "g" Sound

In this sound box story, Little "g" has her own special hard sound. Little "g" has another sound, too. It is soft, like the sound of the letter "j." Can you read these words? Listen for the soft sound.

gem

geranium

gerbil

gingerbread

giraffe

More to Do!

Little 👧 had fun in her garden. You can make your own garden of grassy girls and guys with a little help from an adult.

What you need:

- clean, dry eggshells with the tops removed
- markers
- scraps of paper and cloth
- glue
- potting soil
- grass seeds
- water

Directions:

1. Use your markers to gently draw faces on the eggshells. Be sure each face has a happy grin! Let the faces dry.

2. Use the scraps of paper or cloth to make glasses and goggles for your grinning friends. Use glue to be sure the scraps stick to the eggshells.

3. Fill the shells with potting soil.

4. Sprinkle some grass seeds on top of the soil. Press the seeds down gently.

5. Water the soil just a tiny bit. Place the eggshells in an egg carton (without its top) and set it in a sunny window.

6. Keep the soil moist (but not too wet). In a few days you will have a garden of girls and guys with grassy "hair" that you can trim!

About the Author

Best-selling author Jane Belk Moncure has written over 300 books throughout her teaching and writing career. After earning a Master's degree in Early Childhood Education from Columbia University, she became one of the pioneers in that field. In 1956, she helped form the Virginia Association for Early Childhood Education, which established the first statewide standards for teachers of young children.

Inspired by her work in the classroom, Mrs. Moncure's books have become standards in primary education, and her name is recognized across the country. Her success is reflected not only in her books' popularity with parents, children, and educators, but also by numerous awards, including the 1984 C. S. Lewis Gold Medal Award.

About the Illustrator

Rebecca Thornburgh lives in a pleasantly spooky old house in Philadelphia. If she's not at her drawing table, she's reading—or singing with her band, called Reckless Amateurs. Rebecca has one husband, two daughters, and two silly dogs.

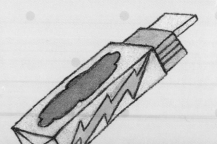